HENRY AND THE BULLY

NANCY CARLSON

PUFFIN BOOKS
An Imprint of Penguin Group (USA) Inc.

To everyone who stands up to bullies by asking
for help. You are cool! Bullies are not!
—NANCY CARLSON

PUFFIN BOOKS
Published by the Penguin Group
Penguin Young Readers Group, 345 Hudson Street, New York, New York 10014, U.S.A.
Penguin Group (Canada), 90 Eglinton Avenue East, Suite 700, Toronto, Ontario, Canada M4P 2Y3 (a division of Pearson Penguin Canada Inc.)
Penguin Books Ltd, 80 Strand, London WC2R 0RL, England
Penguin Ireland, 25 St Stephen's Green, Dublin 2, Ireland (a division of Penguin Books Ltd)
Penguin Group (Australia), 250 Camberwell Road, Camberwell, Victoria 3124, Australia
(a division of Pearson Australia Group Pty Ltd)
Penguin Books India Pvt Ltd, 11 Community Centre, Panchsheel Park, New Delhi - 110 017, India
Penguin Group (NZ), 67 Apollo Drive, Rosedale, Auckland 0632, New Zealand (a division of Pearson New Zealand Ltd.)
Penguin Books (South Africa) (Pty) Ltd, 24 Sturdee Avenue,
Rosebank, Johannesburg 2196, South Africa

Registered Offices: Penguin Books Ltd, 80 Strand, London WC2R 0RL, England

First published in the United States of America by Viking, a division of Penguin Young Readers Group, 2010
Published by Puffin Books, a division of Penguin Young Readers Group, 2012

1 3 5 7 9 10 8 6 4 2

Copyright © Nancy Carlson, 2010
All rights reserved

THE LIBRARY OF CONGRESS HAS CATALOGED THE VIKING EDITION AS FOLLOWS:
Carlson, Nancy.
Henry and the bully / by Nancy Carlson
p.   cm.
Summary: When a new second grader begins bullying Henry and the other first graders,
Henry stumbles onto a secret that just might save them.
ISBN: 978-0-670-01148-3 (hc)
[1. Bullies—Fiction. 2. Mice—Fiction. 3. Animals—Fiction.] I. Title
PZ7.C21665Hcg 2010
[E]—dc22   2009024904

Puffin Books ISBN 978-0-14-242120-8

Manufactured in China

The first graders loved playing soccer during recess.
But one day Henry was chasing the ball when . . .

. . . he ran right into Sam, the new second grader.

A bunch of second graders laughed when
Sam kicked the ball right over the fence!

"Hey, why did you do that?" asked Henry.
"Because I wanted to. You got a problem
with that, Shrimp?" said Sam.

"Uh . . . *no* . . ." said Henry.

After recess, Henry told Mr. McCarthy what
Sam had done. "Sam is a big bully!" said Henry.

"Oh, I know all about bullies," said Mr. McCarthy. "When I was a pup, a bully picked on me.

"Don't worry, I'll keep an eye on Sam and the second graders," said Mr. McCarthy.

But at the next recess, just as the first
graders got their game going . . .

Mr. McCarthy had to rescue a kindergartner from the monkey bars. While he was busy, Sam grabbed Henry's tail just as he was about to score.

The next day during recess, Mr. McCarthy had
to rush a kid with an owie to the nurse.

Sam said, "Shrimp, *we're* playing soccer now,
so get lost!"

For the rest of the day, Henry was miserable
and his tummy hurt.

To make matters worse, he got all
his spelling words wrong.

The next morning Henry said, "Mom, I'm too sick to go to school."

"That's too bad, because today is Saturday!"
said Henry's mom.

"It is? . . . I'm feeling much better now!"
said Henry.

That afternoon, Henry's mom took him
and Pete to the department store.

While his mom was shopping, Henry was wondering
what to do about the bully. Suddenly . . .

there was Sam! "Samantha, that dress
will be perfect for your Uncle Jimmy's
wedding," said Sam's mom.

Sam didn't seem very happy. She looked even less happy when she saw Henry staring right at her.

Now Henry was *really* worried about what Sam would do to him. That night, Henry dreamed he was a superhero . . .

but in the morning, he was still
just Henry the little mouse.

At school on Monday, Sam cornered Henry in the hallway. "Shrimp, if you tell anyone you saw me trying on that dress, I'll kick your soccer ball into space!"

"I wouldn't tell anyone," Henry said. "You looked pretty embarrassed, and it wouldn't be nice." Sam was so surprised she didn't know what to say.

At recess, the first graders were having a good
game when the second graders showed up.
"Oh, no!" said Sidney.

"Why don't you play soccer with us?" Henry asked Sam. "You're on, Shrimp!" said Sam, but she winked at Henry.

Everyone had a ball playing soccer,

and when the bell rang . . .

Mr. McCarthy said, "I see everyone is playing together nicely. I'm glad I could help!"